Hannibal's Noisy Day

Written by
Anne Adeney

Illustrated by
Christina Bretschneider

FRANKLIN WATTS
LONDON•SYDNEY

Anne Adeney

"My favourite pet was 'Rainbow', my chameleon. My four children had lots of pets, too. The hamster was the smallest, and the noisiest!"

Christina Bretschneider

"I live with my two cats, Mimi and Biene. I love drawing all kinds of animals but I have never owned a hamster, yet!"

Wakefield Libraries
& Information Services

This book should be returned by the last date stamped
above. You may renew the loan personally, by post or
telephone for a further period if the book is not required by
another reader.

First published in 2005 by
Franklin Watts
96 Leonard Street
London
EC2A 4XD

Franklin Watts Australia
45–51 Huntley Street
Alexandria
NSW 2015

A CIP catalogue record for this book is available
from the British Library.

ISBN 0 7496 5940 8 (hbk)
ISBN 0 7496 5946 7 (pbk)

Series Editor: Jackie Hamley
Series Advisors: Dr Barrie Wade, Dr Hilary Minn
Design: Peter Scoulding

Printed in Hong Kong / China

For my niece Hanna who loves all kinds of animals! – C.B.

It was morning.

Hannibal the hamster shut
his eyes. "It's time for me
to sleep now."

Then Jacob's alarm clock rang:

COCK-A-DOODLE-DOOOO!

"Be quiet!" said Hannibal.

"I'm trying to sleep!"

9

"Jacob is going to school,"
said Hannibal.

"Time for me to sleep."

Then the postman arrived:
DING-DONG!

"Be quiet!" said Hannibal.

"I'm trying to sleep!"

13

Hannibal shut his eyes. Then
Grandma started cleaning:
BRMM-BRMM!

"Be quiet!" said Hannibal.

"I'm trying to sleep!"

15

Hannibal went to sleep.

Then the baby started to cry:

"WAAH-WAAH!"

"Be quiet!" said Hannibal.

"I'm trying to sleep!"

"I'll sleep now," said Hannibal.

An ambulance went by:

NEE-NAA! NEE-NAA!

"Be quiet!" said Hannibal.

"I'm trying to sleep!"

Later on, Kelly came in.
"Wake up, Hannibal!"
said Kelly. "Let's play!"

"Be quiet!" said Hannibal.

"I'm trying to sleep!"

21

When Dad came home, he cut
the grass: ZROOM-ZROOM!

Then Mum put the radio on:
"LA-LA-LA-LA-LAAAA!"

"BE QUIET!" said Hannibal.

"I'm trying to sleep.

Why are you so *noisy*?"

25

At last, everyone sat down to eat.

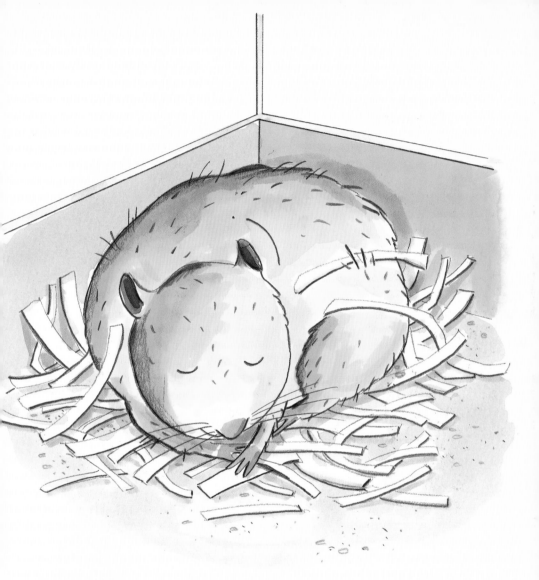

Hannibal could have a good sleep.

When Hannibal woke up,
he saw his wheel.

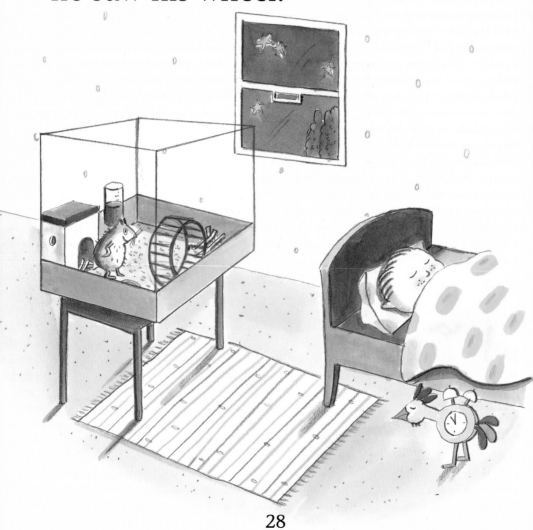

clitter-clatter!

"*I* can play now," he said:

CLITTER-CLATTER!

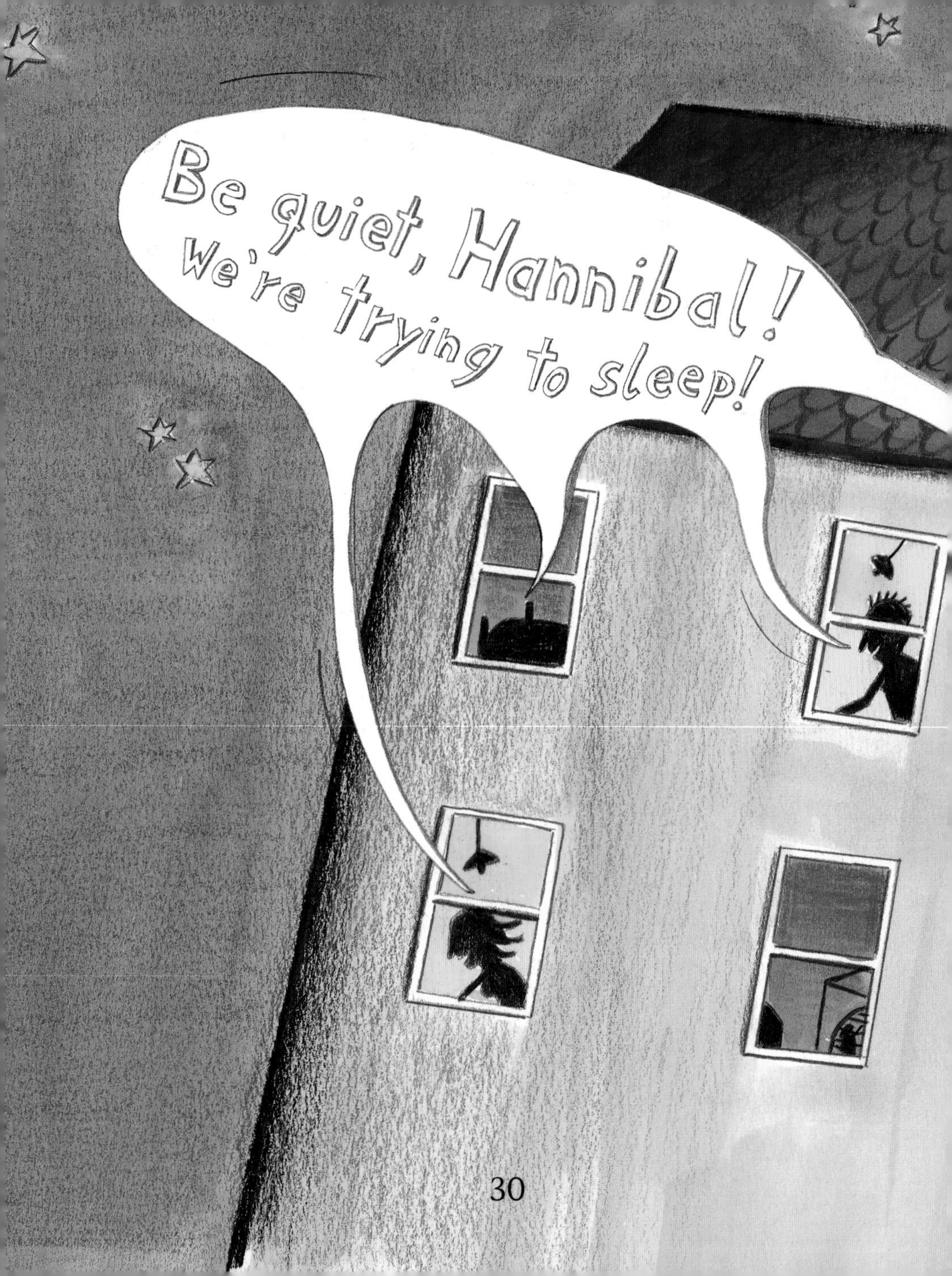
Be quiet, Hannibal!
We're trying to sleep!

Notes for parents and teachers

READING CORNER has been structured to provide maximum support for new readers. The stories may be used by adults for sharing with young children. Primarily, however, the stories are designed for newly independent readers, whether they are reading these books in bed at night, or in the reading corner at school or in the library.

Starting to read alone can be a daunting prospect. READING CORNER helps by providing visual support and repeating words and phrases, while making reading enjoyable. These books will develop confidence in the new reader, and encourage a love of reading that will last a lifetime!

If you are reading this book with a child, here are a few tips:

1. Make reading fun! Choose a time to read when you and the child are relaxed and have time to share the story.

2. Encourage children to reread the story, and to retell the story in their own words, using the illustrations to remind them what has happened.

3. Give praise! Remember that small mistakes need not always be corrected.

READING CORNER covers three grades of early reading ability, with three levels at each grade. Each level has a certain number of words per story, indicated by the number of bars on the spine of the book, to allow you to choose the right book for a young reader:

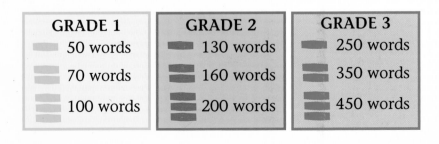

GRADE 1	GRADE 2	GRADE 3
50 words	130 words	250 words
70 words	160 words	350 words
100 words	200 words	450 words